ART FRAUD
DETECTIVE

ANNA NILSEN

KINGFISHER

For Elaine
From ATB

KINGFISHER
a Houghton Mifflin Company imprint
222 Berkeley Street
Boston, Massachusetts 02116
www.houghtonmifflinbooks.com

First published in 2000
6 8 10 9 7

6TR/0103/TWP/MAR(MAR)/150NYM

LIBRARY OF CONGRESS CATALOGING-IN-PUBLICATION DATA
Bassil, Andrea.
Art fraud detective / by Andrea Bassil.—1st ed.
p. cm.
Summary: A spot-the-difference game, mystery story, and art book in which readers
try to tell which paintings are genuine and which are forgeries. Includes magnifying glass
and split-page format.
ISBN 0-7534-5308-8
1. Painting—Forgeries—Juvenile literature. 2. Toy and movable books—Specimens.
[1. Painting. 2. Art appreciation. 3. Picture puzzles. 4. Toy and movable books.] I. Title.
ND1660 .B38 2000
751.5'8—dc21
00-027059

Printed in Singapore

Author and forgery artwork: Anna Nilsen
Illustrator: Andy Parker
Editor: Camilla Reid
Senior Designer: Sarah Goodwin

The Publishers would also like to thank the following:
Sinead and Rowan Derbyshire, Elaine Ward,
Erika Langmuir, and Suzie Burt.

THE MYSTERY CALLER

At the Museum of Art, Mr. Bassett, the old security guard, receives a phone call from someone with a strange, muffled voice. It looks like the gallery may have a bit of a problem....

RING! RING!

ZZZ

Hello?

Mr. Bassett? I have some very important information that could save your museum from total disaster!

What the...! Who is this?

You silly old fool, you call yourself a security guard?! THIRTY of your paintings have been stolen from under your nose—by four notorious gangs of forgers—and replaced by cunning FAKES! If you want to catch the forgers and stop the real paintings from being sold on the black market...

...you'd better find the fakes, FAST! You want to know who I am? All I can tell you is that I am a member of one of the gangs, but I've had enough of life as a criminal. Of all the forgers, I was the only one who refused to get involved in the Museum of Art job.

For my own safety, I'm keeping my identity secret and staying in disguise until those devious villains are locked up behind bars. However, if you're smart, you may be able to figure out my identity. Oh, one last thing...each gang member, apart from me, has forged exactly TWO paintings!

...and then the line goes dead.

This is a catastrophe for the Museum of Art! If we go to the experts for help, people will find out that our paintings aren't the real thing—we'll have to close down and the masterpieces will be lost forever.

But, hang on...if I had a quick, clever private detective to search the museum and find the forgeries, we could still save it. I've got an idea! How about...

YOU?

FACTS FOR THE DETECTIVE

Are you ready to accept the challenge? If you are, then there are a few things you need to know before you start. First of all, the Museum of Art holds a total of thirty-four pictures. Starting at the entrance, you should work through the collection, looking at the paintings one by one. Remember what the mystery caller said—thirty of them are fakes!

INSIDE THE MUSEUM OF ART

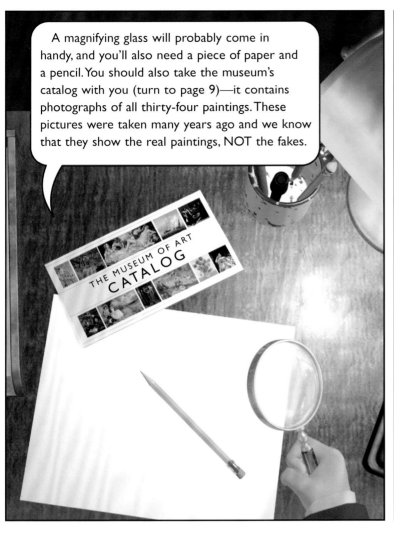

A magnifying glass will probably come in handy, and you'll also need a piece of paper and a pencil. You should also take the museum's catalog with you (turn to page 9)—it contains photographs of all thirty-four paintings. These pictures were taken many years ago and we know that they show the real paintings, NOT the fakes.

Now, I must confess that I've known about these forgers for a little while. This letter arrived from the police the other day, but I'm afraid that I hadn't paid much attention to it until now.

TO ART MUSEUMS WORLDWIDE:
FORGER ALERT!
ISSUED BY THE INTERNATIONAL POLICE ALLIANCE

Four gangs of art forgers are known to be operating internationally. Each gang has four members who work as a team, dividing the profits of their crimes between them. The gangs are fierce rivals and compete with each other to steal paintings from museums around the world, replacing them with worthless forgeries. Unfortunately, not enough evidence has been found yet to convict the forgers. THEY ARE STILL ON THE LOOSE—BE ON GUARD!

5

The police also sent me a poster that shows the four gangs of forgers. I've pinned it to my bulletin board and you should take a closer look at it. I have a feeling that it will be very useful in helping you find out which are the fake paintings, and who forged them.

Turn to the next page to see the poster close up...

ART FRAUD

ISSUED TO ART MUSEUMS WORLDWIDE BY THE INTERNATIONAL POLICE ALLIANCE

Each gang of forgers is secretly proud of its work and stamps all
its fakes with a particular symbol, hidden somewhere in the painting.
The International Police Alliance has also discovered that each forger
makes a set number of deliberate, tiny changes to every painting

FISH GANG

Name: Molly Mullet
Number of changes: 1

Name: Claude Conger
Number of changes: 2

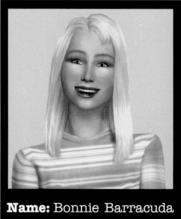

Name: Bonnie Barracuda
Number of changes: 3

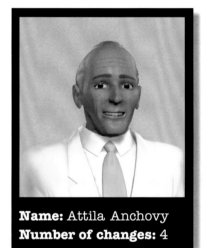

Name: Attila Anchovy
Number of changes: 4

BIRD GANG

Name: Genghis Gull
Number of changes: 1

Name: Lizzie Lapwing
Number of changes: 2

Name: Hawley Hornbill
Number of changes: 3

Name: Imelda Ibis
Number of changes: 4

SUSPECTS

that he or she forges. Each forger always makes exactly the same number of changes—their "signature." **By locating the hidden symbol and counting the changes, it is possible to identify the forger who made each fake**. The gangs and their members are as follows:

STAR GANG

Name: Portia Pollux
Number of changes: 1

Name: Bugsy Betelgeuse
Number of changes: 2

Name: Saffron Sirius
Number of changes: 3

Name: Vasile Vega
Number of changes: 4

TREE GANG

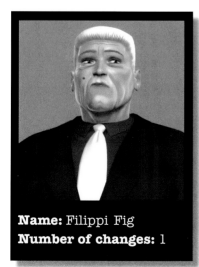

Name: Filippi Fig
Number of changes: 1

Name: Annie Apricot
Number of changes: 2

Name: Josef Juniper
Number of changes: 3

Name: Salome Spruce
Number of changes: 4

LOOK FOR THE CLUES!

It's time to start your detective work

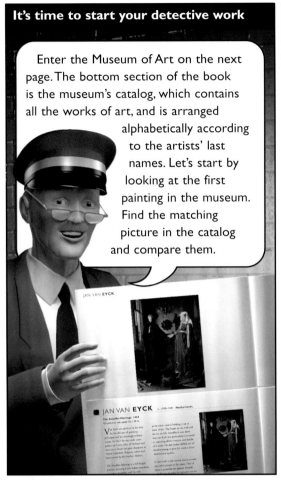

Enter the Museum of Art on the next page. The bottom section of the book is the museum's catalog, which contains all the works of art, and is arranged alphabetically according to the artists' last names. Let's start by looking at the first painting in the museum. Find the matching picture in the catalog and compare them.

If the picture is a forgery, it will contain a hidden symbol and between one and four changes…I've found a tree symbol! So, this picture has been forged by a member of the Tree Gang. I can also see that the forger has added another shoe, removed the beads, and changed the color of the woman's waistband. So there are three changes in total.

Now turn back to the Art Fraud Suspects poster. By matching the tree symbol with three changes, I can deduce that Josef Juniper forged the painting by Jan van Eyck.

SUSPECTS

that he or she forges. Each forger always makes exactly the same number of changes—their "signature." By locating the hidden symbol and counting the changes, it is possible to identify the forger who made each fake. The gangs and their members are as follows:

STAR GANG ★

| Name: Portia Picture | Name: Bugsy Betelgeuse | Name: Saffron Sirius | Name: Vanilla Vega |
| Number of changes: 1 | Number of changes: 2 | Number of changes: 3 | Number of changes: 4 |

TREE GANG ♣

| Name: Filippo Fig | Name: Adolst Apricot | Name: Josef Juniper | Name: Salome Spruce |
| Number of changes: 1 | Number of changes: 2 | Number of changes: 3 | Number of changes: 4 |

Draw a chart like this. Fill in the artist and the forger as you find them. If you discover a real painting, write it down in the bottom section. The mystery caller did not do any forgeries, so his or her name will not be on the chart.

GANG SYMBOL / NUMBER OF CHANGES	FISH GANG 🐟	BIRD GANG ✈	STAR GANG ★	TREE GANG 🌴
1				
2				VAN EYCK Josef Juniper
3				
4				
REAL PAINTINGS (no changes)	1.	2.	3.	4.

Your mission is to…

1. Find the four real paintings.

2. Find out who made each fake. (Remember, every forger, except for the mystery caller, has made two fakes.)

3. Identify the mystery caller (the only name not on your chart!)

GOOD LUCK!

If you need some help, turn to page 45.
The answers are on pages 46–47, but don't cheat!

8

TO THE PAINTINGS

JAN VAN **EYCK**

THE MUSEUM OF ART
CATALOG

HENDRICK **AVERCAMP** 1585–1634 **Holland**

A Winter Scene with Skaters near a Castle 1608 or 1609

Oil paint on oak panel 16 1/2 x 16 1/2 in.

Profoundly deaf, and unable to speak, Avercamp was known as "the mute of Kampen." He specialized in finely detailed winter scenes, filled with movement and dotted with a lot of tiny figures. Although he painted cold, snowy scenes, he usually used a palette of warm colors, such as pink and brown, in his pictures.

The buildings in *A Winter Scene with Skaters near a Castle* are painted from the imagination, but the skaters and toboganners are based on watercolor drawings made from life. Returning to his studio, Avercamp would use his sketches to create his carefully composed paintings, grouping the figures, holding hands and dancing, to make patterns within the picture. In this scene, we can see that because of the freezing weather, all work—fishing, farming, and brewing, for example—has stopped and everyone, rich and poor, is out on the ice having fun.

SANDRO **BOTTICELLI** 1445–1510 **Italy**

Venus and Mars 1485

Tempera and oil paint on poplar panel 27 ½ x 69 ½ in.

Botticelli worked mainly in Florence, painting religious pictures and portraits for his patrons, the powerful Medici family. He also decorated the walls of the Sistine Chapel in the Vatican in Rome (the famous ceiling of which was painted twenty years later by Michelangelo).

In *Venus and Mars*, Venus, the goddess of love, sits watching her sleeping lover, Mars, the god of war. Even the sound of a trumpet in his ear does not wake him, and the satyrs (mythical creatures that are half-goat, half-human) are able to playfully steal his lance. This beautifully detailed picture was probably used as a bedroom decoration, either for the wall or as part of a piece of furniture.

JAN **BRUEGHEL** 1568–1625 **Belgium**

The Adoration of the Kings 1598

Watercolor on leather 13 x 19 in.

Jan Brueghel was the youngest son in a family of famous painters, led by his father Pieter Brueghel. Jan Brueghel usually painted flower pictures, landscapes, and small, finely detailed paintings of people. He gave his pictures such a polished finish that he earned the nickname "Velvet Brueghel."

The Adoration of the Kings shows the three kings bringing gifts to the baby Jesus. King Balthazar stands on the right carrying a golden ship. Brueghel chose to set the painting in his own time, and placed the rickety old stable in a busy town, surrounded by people and animals going about their daily business.

HENDRICK TER **BRUGGHEN** 1588–1629 **Holland**

The Concert 1626

Oil paint on canvas 39 ½ x 46 ½ in.

Ter Brugghen lived in Italy for ten years and became an admirer of the work of the master painter Caravaggio. He liked the way in which Caravaggio used dark shadows and bright highlights to create mood in his paintings. Ter Brugghen borrowed this technique for his gentle, atmospheric pictures.

The mood of *The Concert* is one of warmth, closeness, and just a little mystery. Three musicians face each other in a ring, lit by a low candle. This gives the faces a golden glow, but at the same time casts strange, dancing shadows on the wall behind them. The young boy focuses on his book, beating out the rhythm of the music with his hand, lost in his own world. The other two musicians seem to be aware of us looking at them. The candlelight catches their eyes as they glance out toward us— but they keep their backs turned, shutting us out of their circle.

JEAN-BAPTISTE-SIMEON **CHARDIN** 1699–1779 **France**

The House of Cards c. 1735

Oil paint on canvas 24 x 29 in.

Like the Dutch painter de Hooch, Chardin liked to capture the lives of ordinary people in his paintings. His pictures were often bought by royalty and members of the upper classes who enjoyed them for their simplicity and calmness.

The boy in *The House of Cards* is probably the son of a friend of Chardin's named Monsieur Le Noir, who was a Parisian cabinetmaker. It seems likely that Monsieur Le Noir was successful in his work because his son is dressed in expensive clothes and is able to idle his time away playing cards. It is a natural scene, in which the boy seems unaware of the painter's presence and gives his full concentration to the game. In this painting, Chardin used thick brushstrokes in layers. Up close, they seem blurred and careless. From a distance, however, they take shape and give the picture a warm, still quality.

JOHN **CONSTABLE** 1776–1837 **England**

The Haywain 1821

Oil paint on canvas 52 x 74 in.

The son of a mill owner, Constable grew up in the county of Suffolk. As an adult he lived in London, but often returned to his home county to paint the countryside he had known as a child.

Constable's landscapes often have as their subject the harmony between human beings and nature. *The Haywain* is a peaceful scene, which shows an empty hay wagon (haywain) in the Stour River, next to a house known as Willy Lott's Cottage. In the distance, workers are cutting the hay. Constable's great skill lay in the way he captured the tiny movements of nature—the tops of the trees shimmering in the breeze and the shadows of the clouds dancing across the meadow.

EDGAR **DEGAS**   1834–1917 **France**

Miss La La at the Cirque Fernando 1879

Oil paint on canvas 47 x 31 in.

Degas was born in Paris, the son of a rich banker. As a young man, he studied law, but later chose to go to art school instead. Around 1865, he became friendly with a group of artists now known as the Impressionists, and ten of his paintings were shown at their first exhibition, in 1874. Although he is now known as an Impressionist, Degas' work was in many ways very different from the rest of the group's. While they tended to paint in the open air, capturing moments as they happened, Degas was interested in indoor scenes, making detailed sketches before returning to his studio to paint.

Degas particularly loved theatrical and sporting subjects, especially scenes of ballet dancers and racehorses, and often depicted ordinary people working and bathing. *Miss La La at the Cirque Fernando* captures the famous Parisian acrobat as she dangles from a rope clenched between her teeth. This extraordinary feat of strength caused a sensation at the time and Degas catches this breathtaking moment by painting it from the point of view of a member of the audience. The strange diagonals of the arms, legs, and rafters, and the strong, yellow lighting all add to the drama and suspense of the scene.

PAUL **DELAROCHE** 1795–1856 **France**

The Execution of Lady Jane Grey 1833

Oil paint on canvas 98 1/2 x 119 in.

Delaroche painted historical subjects and was one of the most popular French painters of the early 1800s.

Lady Jane Grey was the great-granddaughter of Henry VII and, following the death of Edward VI in 1553, she became Queen of England, at the age of seventeen. Only nine days long, her reign was one of the shortest in history—she was deposed by supporters of Mary Tudor and found guilty of treason. *The Execution of Lady Jane Grey* shows Lady Jane as she is guided blindfold to the block. Sir John Brydges, Lieutenant of the Tower of London, talks softly to her as the executioner waits, axe in hand. To the left, her ladies-in-waiting grieve. It is a powerful, dramatic picture, in which the dark background contrasts starkly with the pale, fragile figure of Lady Jane, just moments before her life was ended.

JAN VAN **EYCK** c. 1390–1441 **Netherlands**

The Arnolfini Marriage 1434

Oil paint on oak panel 33 x 24 in.

Van Eyck was admired in his time for his delicate oil painting technique and his amazingly realistic scenes. In 1422, he was made court painter to Count John of Holland and went on to finish the great altarpiece at Ghent Cathedral, Belgium, which had been started by his brother, Hubert.

The Arnolfini Marriage is a full-length portrait, showing a rich Italian merchant, Giovanni Arnolfini and his wife, who lived in Bruges at the time. Although she looks as if she is pregnant, she is in fact wearing a very long dress—in fashion at the time—and is holding it up in front of her. The beads on the wall and the fur on Mr. Arnolfini's coat show that van Eyck was particularly interested in capturing all the textures and details of a scene. He also makes skillful use of foreshortening to give the room a three-dimensional quality.

A close look at the concave mirror reveals two other people in the room. One of them is probably the painter himself, and this ties in with his signature on the back wall, which, when translated, reads "Jan van Eyck was here 1434."

THOMAS **GAINSBOROUGH** 1727–88 **England**

Mr. and Mrs. Andrews 1748–49

Oil paint on canvas 28 x 47 ½ in.

It is claimed that Gainsborough once said, "I hate painting portraits. I want to paint landskips [landscapes]." Even so, he painted over two hundred portraits, usually of fashionable members of society.

Mr. and Mrs. Andrews is both a portrait and a landscape. It was probably commissioned by the couple the year after their marriage, and shows them on their country estate in late summer, as the harvest is being gathered. Gainsborough may have intended Mrs. Andrews to be holding a dead pheasant in her lap, but this part of the picture remains unfinished.

VINCENT VAN **GOGH** 1853–90 **Holland**

Sunflowers 1888

Oil paint on canvas 37 x 29 in.

Van Gogh worked as an art dealer, a teacher, and a missionary before becoming an artist at the late age of 27. He is now considered to be one of the world's greatest painters, despite having very little training as an artist and only selling one picture during his lifetime.

An anxious, often tormented person, Van Gogh spent the rest of his life trying to understand the world—and his place in it—through his art. He was afflicted by periods of madness, and is famous for cutting off part of his ear during one of them. He was influenced by the Impressionists, but went on to develop his own very individual style of painting, which is known as Postimpressionism.

Van Gogh worked energetically, using paint straight from the tube and laying it on in thick brushstrokes. In *Sunflowers,* he uses this technique to give texture to the seed heads and to make the petals radiate a vibrant warmth. Van Gogh loved sunflowers for their simple shape and brilliant colors. He painted a number of similar paintings to decorate a room in his house that was often used by Paul Gauguin, his friend and fellow painter.

JAN **GOSSAERT**   c. 1503–32 **Netherlands**

A Little Girl 1520

Oil paint on oak panel 15 x 10 in.

Gossaert was an engraver who painted religious and mythological subjects, as well as portraits. In 1508, he visited Italy, and was inspired by the new type of art that he saw being produced by Renaissance artists. Returning to the Netherlands, he became widely admired by his fellow painters and also gained many rich patrons across Europe.

Although the identity of the little girl in this portrait is not known for certain, she may have been Jacqueline, the youngest daughter of Adolphe de Bourgogne and Anne de Bergues, patrons of Gossaert.

Her pearl-encrusted clothes and fine gold jewelry tell us that her family was extremely wealthy and probably held an important place in society.

Using an unusual optical illusion, Gossaert places the girl in front of an imaginary picture frame. In her hand is an astronomical instrument called an armillary sphere, designed to show the movement of the planets. Curiously, she is holding it upside down, which suggests that although someone in her family is well educated, she herself has not yet learned how to use it correctly.

HANS **HOLBEIN** c. 1497–1543 **Germany**

The Ambassadors 1533

Oil paint on wood panel 83 x 84 in.

During the 1500s, Europe became bitterly divided by a religious revolution known as the Reformation. Like many artists, Holbein was unable to make a living in Germany and so moved to London, England. A few years later he became court painter to King Henry VIII.

The Ambassadors is a portrait of two French diplomats who visited Henry VIII's court in 1533. Their clothes and the objects around them show that these men are highly educated, powerful, and wealthy. Each object has been selected to give the painting meaning. The instruments on the upper shelf are for examining the stars and measuring dates and time. They contrast with the objects on the lower shelf, which relate to human life on earth. The skull-shaped badge and the broken lute string remind us that we will all die, while the crucifix in the top left corner adds the hope of life after death. Look closely at the floor and you will see a strange object. Try looking at it from another angle—can you figure out what it is?

PIETER DE **HOOCH** 1629–84 **Holland**

The Courtyard of a House in Delft 1658

Oil paint on canvas 29 1/2 x 24 in.

Pieter de Hooch was a painter of portraits and small, detailed scenes of everyday life. His pictures usually show women and children enjoying simple pastimes or carrying out tasks around the home. This painting is set in a prosperous part of the Dutch city of Delft and is probably based on a real house. A maid and child walk down the steps talking to each other, while in the passageway, a woman stands looking out into the street. De Hooch's paintings reflect his belief that children should be brought up with care, in neat, quiet surroundings.

The perspective of the picture is carefully thought out and is designed to lead the eye through the passageway, to the delicately lit background of the street beyond. The picture has a number of clear lines, with strong horizontals (the steps, the brickwork, and the flagstones), and verticals (the doorways, passage, and corner). These give the painting structure and balance, reflecting the well-ordered lives of the people depicted in it. The use of soft, muted tones, and a small range of colors—mainly oranges and browns—also helps to create an atmosphere of harmony.

Madame Moitessier 1856

Oil paint on canvas 37 x 29 in.

Ingres deeply admired the art of ancient Greece and Rome and spent his life trying to achieve the simple lines and finely modeled shapes found in Classical art. Because of this, he was known as a Neoclassicist, which means "new classicist."

Even though he painted many portraits, Ingres preferred capturing scenes from famous myths and historical events. At first, he turned down the commission to paint Madame Moitessier, but on meeting her, he was struck by her classical beauty and changed his mind.

Her marble-smooth skin and calm gaze reminds us of a classical statue. But Madame Moitessier was also a real person, and by looking closely at the painting we can learn some things about her. We know that she was the wife of a successful French banker. The richly decorated room, her heavy gold jewelry, and extravagant, fashionable dress show that the couple was indeed very wealthy. And by painting her against a mirror, Ingres makes sure that we see every detail of her grand setting. Surrounded by luxury and waited on by servants, she probably led a life of comfort and ease.

LEONARDO DA VINCI 1452–1519 **Italy**

The Virgin and Child with Saint Anne and Saint John the Baptist 1499–1500

Charcoal and black and white chalk on tinted paper 57 x 42 in.

With an endless curiosity and a hunger for knowledge, Leonardo da Vinci was certainly one of the greatest geniuses the world has ever seen. Not only was he a superb artist, but he also had an exceptional understanding of nature and science. He was so eager to understand the human body that he dissected corpses in order to study and draw anatomy. Although he made thousands of notes and drawings in his studies of the natural world, only fifteen of his paintings survive today, the most famous of which is the *Mona Lisa*.

This cartoon shows the Virgin Mary seated on the knee of her mother, St. Anne, while holding the Christ Child, who is blessing Saint John the Baptist. The figures are intertwined both physically and emotionally, and there is a great sense of tenderness about the group. Leonardo was a master at using light and shade to give his paintings and drawings relief (three dimensions). The detail in the darkest shadows and brightest highlights gives the faces a mysterious radiance and almost makes it seem possible to reach out and touch the clothes.

MARINUS VAN REYMERSWAELE   1509–67 **Netherlands**

Two Tax Gatherers 1540

Oil paint on oak paint 37 x 29 ½ in.

Little is known of the life of Marinus van Reymerswaele. We know that he is named after the town of Reimerswaal, an area that is now covered by sea. We also know that he studied drawings by Leonardo da Vinci and that, like Leonardo, he was a gifted painter of caricatures (portraits that exaggerate the features for comic effect). He was admired in his day for his satirical paintings—works that mercilessly mock different aspects of human nature, such as greed and laziness. His pictures often feature imaginary portraits of corrupt bankers and tax collectors.

Two Tax Gatherers shows a mean-looking town treasurer (on the left), writing out a list of taxes. His hideous companion looks on greedily, his distorted, grasping hands reaching out toward the pile of coins in front of them. Both rogues are dressed in fantastic, elaborate costumes that exaggerate their wicked characters. Behind them is a shelf so overcrowded with bundles of paper, boxes, and books that some of them are tumbling onto the floor—a sign that these are not honest, hardworking businessmen. Ignoring the chaos, the men are concerned only with counting the money.

QUINTEN **MASSYS** 1465–1530 **Netherlands**

A Grotesque Old Woman c. 1525

Oil paint on oak panel 25 1/2 x 18 in.

Massys painted portraits and religious altarpieces and was regarded as the leading painter in Antwerp. His early work was influenced by the refined, realistic style of van Eyck. However, after making a trip to Italy, his later works show that he was almost certainly familiar with drawings of grotesque figures by Leonardo da Vinci. In fact, the painting of *A Grotesque Old Woman* seems to be based on one of Leonardo's drawings.

This was probably not a portrait of a real woman, but was designed to criticize older women who do not accept their age and try to look younger than they actually are. Because she has not faced the truth of her age, Massys deliberately makes his subject look grotesque and foolish. It is thought that the English illustrator Sir John Tenniel drew on Massys' old woman for the Duchess in Lewis Carroll's *Alice in Wonderland*. Massys also did several portraits of old men in this style, which may have been inspired by the great humanist Erasmus. Massys had met and painted portraits of Erasmus, and read his writings, including *In Praise of Folly* (published 1512).

CLAUDE **MONET**   1840–1926 **France**

The Gare St.-Lazare 1877

Oil paint on canvas 21 1/2 x 29 1/2 in.

Monet was one of a group of painters known as the Impressionists that worked in France in the second half of the 1800s. Although exceptionally popular now, the work of these painters puzzled the public and critics when it was first seen.

Painted on the spot, *The Gare St.-Lazare* is like a snapshot—an impression—of a moment in time. Monet worked quickly, using loose strokes of color, with no outlines or solid forms. His aim was to capture the light and atmosphere of the railroad station rather than its tiny details. As a result, it is easy to feel as though you are standing in the station with the other passengers as the huge, noisy train pulls in to the platform, surrounded by billowing clouds of steam.

BERTHE **MORISOT** 1841–1895 **France**

Summer's Day c. 1879

Oil paint on canvas 18 1/2 x 30 in.

Morisot was born in Bourges, in central France, but moved to Paris with her family when she was eleven. One of very few female artists of international fame, Morisot is best known for her scenes of modern life. She worked in oils, pastels, and watercolors, showing landscapes and everyday scenes. She knew the Impressionists, and *Summer's Day* was shown in their fifth exhibition in 1880, under the title *The Lake in the Bois de Boulogne*. It is a peaceful, still scene that shows two middle-class, city women relaxing in a rowboat. The lake is set in a fashionable park to the west of Paris, where people would go for picnics and to walk in the gardens.

JAN VAN OS   1744–1808 Holland

Fruit and Flowers in a Terracotta Vase 1777–78

Oil paint on mahogany panel 35 1/2 x 28 1/2 in.

Jan van Os was the head of a family of artists who specialized in still lifes of fruit and flowers.

Although it is a still life, *Fruit and Flowers in a Terracotta Vase* is overflowing with movement and energy. The tower of fruit and flowers seems to be about to topple over. Bursting with colors and textures, the painting is a glorious celebration of the natural world—and the skill of the painter. Set against a grand temple background, grapes, plums, and a pineapple are packed together with roses, carnations, tulips, and even a number of tiny creatures such as butterflies. The detail is so fine that we feel we could reach out and feel the dewy petals or the pin-sharp thorns.

It comes as a surprise to learn, that this is an extremely artificial composition. A clue to this lies in the bottom left-hand corner, which tells us that the painting took over a year to complete. The fruit and flowers that van Os painted ripen and bloom at different times of the year. He would have had to wait for each one to come into season before he could capture it accurately in paint.

JEAN-BAPTISTE **PERRONNEAU** 1715–83 **France**

A Girl with a Kitten 1745

Pastel on paper 23 1/2 x 20 in.

The use of pastel as a medium for paintings became fashionable in France in the 1700s after the Venetian artist Rosalba Carriera visited Paris in 1720–21. She was one of the first to work in pastels—dry, chalky sticks made by mixing pure pigment, for the color, with a little gum to bind them. The paintings she created were admired for their decorative quality.

Perronneau had studied engraving, but was clearly influenced by Carriera's work and became well known in France for his pastel portraits. With pastels, he was able to use color to show light and shade in a subtle way.

No one knows who the little girl in this painting is. We can guess that her family was prosperous and held a high position in society. Although she is still a child, she seems to be dressed in adult's clothes, and, like all fashionable people at the time, has powdered hair. This is because, in the 1700s, children were treated like adults from an early age. At about the age of eight, for example, children were expected to give up storybooks in favor of adult literature.

PABLO **PICASSO** 1881–1973 **Spain**

Fruit Dish, Bottle, and Violin 1914

Oil paint on canvas 37 × 29 in.

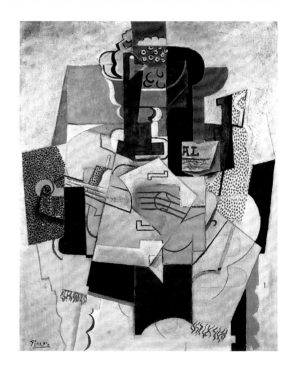

Born in Spain, Picasso was the son of an art teacher named José Blasco. Although he realized that young Pablo was a talented painter, Blasco could not have known that his son would become one of the greatest artists of the 1900s.

As a young man, Picasso painted scenes of circuses and city life. Although these were realistic paintings, Picasso found the people and places around him made him feel sad and lonely, so he painted many of them using only different shades of blue. This time in his life is known as his "Blue Period."

As the years passed, Picasso experimented with new styles of painting and sculpture, and became fascinated by African art. He also worked with another painter, Georges Braque, and together they developed a new form of art called Cubism.

Like many Cubist paintings, *Fruit Dish, Bottle, and Violin* is difficult to understand at first. The objects are not realistic and the picture looks messy. This is because rather than just painting what he saw with his eyes, Picasso used his imagination to try to show the object from many different points of view.

PIERO DELLA FRANCESCA c. 1415–92 Italy

The Baptism of Christ 1450s

Tempera on poplar panel 67 x 46 1/2 in.

Although many people admire his work now, Piero della Francesca was not famous in his lifetime. This may have been because, unlike other Renaissance painters, Piero did not live in Florence, the artistic capital of Italy. Instead, he chose to stay in his hometown of Borgo Sansepolcro for most of his life.

Piero, like most artists of the period, painted religious subjects, and liked to use pale, flat colors to give his work a sense of calm and balance. He was very interested in geometry and perspective, and his paintings are carefully composed.

The Baptism of Christ is a scene from the New Testament of the Bible and shows Jesus being baptized by John the Baptist. A dove, the symbol of the Holy Spirit, hovers overhead, while, to the left, three angels stand holding Christ's clothes. To the right of St. John, a man preparing to be baptized gets undressed, and behind him are four priests. One of them points to the holy light that illuminates the far left-hand tree. This story is described in the Bible as taking place beside the River Jordan, but the landscape of Piero's painting looks more like scenery around Borgo Sansepolcro than the Middle East.

RAPHAEL   1483–1520 **Italy**

Pope Julius II 1511–12

Oil paint on wood 43 x 32 ½ in.

Along with Leonardo da Vinci and Michelangelo, Raphael was one of the masters of the Renaissance, and together, these three artists changed the course of art history.

A skilled artist from a very young age, Raphael tried a number of different art forms. He painted several huge frescoes in churches, a number of altarpieces, and portraits, as well as finding the time to design tapestries and buildings. During his life, he worked throughout Italy and was supported by a number of wealthy patrons, including two popes.

This is a portrait of Pope Julius II, shortly before his death, wearing a red and white cape called a mozzetta to show he is an important figure in the Catholic Church. The pope had grown a beard to show that he was upset about the loss of the city of Bologna. His gloomy face and slumped shoulders show how dejected he felt. The acorns on the chair are emblems of the Pope's family. Raphael originally included the cross-keys (symbols of the pope) as a pattern on the green curtain. He later changed his mind and removed them. Can you spot where they were?

REMBRANDT VAN RIJN   1606–69 Holland

Belshazzar's Feast 1636–38

Oil paint on canvas 67 x 83 ½ in.

Rembrandt was an original, adventurous painter. He had an amazing knack for capturing the personalities of the people he painted, showing what they were feeling and thinking as well as what they looked like.

Belshazzar's Feast catches a dramatic moment in the biblical story of Belshazzar, the king of Babylon. Belshazzar is holding a grand feast and is serving wine in vessels stolen from the temple in Jerusalem. A hand appears from the shadows and writes a message of doom on the wall, warning the king that he will die because he has sinned against God. That same night, Belshazzar dies. Rembrandt has cleverly left much of the room in darkness, highlighting the faces of the horrified spectators. This adds to the suspense, creating an atmosphere of fear and dread.

HENRI **ROUSSEAU**   1844–1910 **France**

Tiger in a Tropical Storm 1891

Oil paint on canvas 52 × 65 in.

Rousseau was a self-taught painter who was known as "Le Douanier" (the customs officer) because he worked at a customs house and only painted in his spare time. He was one of several artists to search for a new way of looking at the world and to be influenced by African sculpture and children's paintings. He was discovered by Picasso.

Rousseau is best known for the paintings that he created from his imagination. *Tiger in a Tropical Storm* is a bold, richly colorful picture that appears to be quite simple in its design. In fact, it is very carefully composed for dramatic effect, with windblown grasses and branches silhouetted against the stormy sky. Rousseau imagined that the tiger was hunting for explorers and first called the painting *Surpris!* (which means "surprised" in French).

GEORGES **SEURAT** 1859–1891 **France**

Bathers at Asnières 1884

Oil paint on canvas 80 ½ x 120 in.

Seurat was an important Postimpressionist painter who spent most of his life working in Paris. He used complementary colors (such as blue and orange, and red and green) side by side to give his work a vibrant feel. Later in his life, he developed pointillism, a technique that uses small dots of color to create an effect.

Seurat usually worked in the open air and was one of the first artists to consider ordinary people important enough to paint on a large canvas. Showing factory workers relaxing on the riverbanks near Paris, this painting is a huge picture with a still, majestic mood.

HARMEN **STEENWYCK** 1612–1655 **Holland**

Still Life: An Allegory of the Vanities of Human Life   c. 1640

Oil paint on oak panel   15 ¹/₂ x 20 ¹/₂ in.

At first glance, this seems to be a rather strange picture. Why would anyone want to paint a skull and a group of other odd things, you might wonder. The answer is that Steenwyck chose each object in this painting very deliberately in order to make us think about death and the importance of living our lives in a useful way.

Many of the objects refer to things that people enjoy during their life on earth. The shell and the Japanese sword would have been very rare in Holland in the 1600s, and they represent wealth. The books are symbols of knowledge and the musical instruments stand for pleasure. Contrasting with them are the reminders of the passing of time and death—the watch counting the hours as they disappear, the recently blown-out lamp, and the skull.

JOSEPH TURNER 1775–1851 England

The Fighting "Temeraire" tugged to her Last Berth to be broken up 1838

Oil paint on canvas 36 1/2 x 49 in.

Turner was one of the first artists to work outdoors. He was fascinated by the power of nature and wanted to show its moods and drama in his paintings. His style was revolutionary and although some people admired his work, others did not understand it at all.

The "Temeraire" was a famous ship that had helped to win the Battle of Trafalgar in 1805. The painting shows the ship as she makes her last voyage before being broken up for salvage. Turner's brilliant sunset bathes her in light, celebrating her glorious victory. The golden sky contrasts with the dark, modern tug that pulls the majestic old ship to her deathbed. The result is a picture that is both joyful and gloomy in feeling.

PAOLO **UCCELLO** 1397–1475 **Italy**

The Battle of San Romano c. 1450–60

Tempera on poplar wood 73 x 128 in.

As a young man, Uccello worked on stained-glass windows and mosaics, which helps explain why *The Battle of San Romano* is such a decorative painting. The picture commemorates the battle between the Italian city-states of Florence and Siena. Making clever use of perspective, Uccello places a dead knight and a number of other objects in the foreground. They are foreshortened and positioned to create a sense of distance and to lead the eye away into the background landscape, far beyond the hedge. The whole effect is increased by the way in which the lances become smaller as they get farther away.

WILLEM VAN DE **VELDE**   1633–1707 **Holland**

A Dutch Ship, a Yacht, and Smaller Vessels in a Breeze c. 1660

Oil paint on canvas 13 x 15 in.

Willem van de Velde came from a family of painters. Like his father, he loved ships and became one of the most acclaimed marine painters in Holland. Although the family settled for a while in Amsterdam, they became very poor after the French invasion and had to move to England to make a living. But their fortunes soon changed, and father and son were made official painters to King Charles II. They were paid a handsome yearly fee of £100 each, Willem for coloring and his father for drawing.

As well as being rich in detail, this painting cleverly captures the feeling of ships at sea as they are buffeted by the wind and waves. The Dutch ship named in the title is a *kaag*, shown in the foreground to the right. The central ship is a States yacht. It is flying the Dutch flag and has the coat of arms of the Province of Holland on its stern. The largest ship on the left-hand side is a *weyschuit*, a Dutch open boat.

JAN **VERMEER** 1632–75 **Holland**

A Young Woman seated at a Virginal c. 1670

Oil paint on canvas 21 x 18 ½ in.

Vermeer lived in the Dutch city of Delft, working as an innkeeper and art dealer to support his large family. It seems that he did not have much time to paint, because only 35 of his pictures survive today. Like de Hooch's scenes, Vermeer's paintings are small and delightfully realistic, showing people going about their lives in and around their homes.

In *A Young Woman seated at a Virginal*, Vermeer invites us to peek around the curtain and join the peaceful, private world of this wealthy young woman.

Seated at a virginal (a keyboard instrument similar to a harpsichord), she seems to look at us as we enter the room but, unconcerned, carries on playing. We notice that propped against the virginal is a viola da gamba. With its player missing, perhaps Vermeer imagined that the viewer would join the young woman in a duet and so complete the scene.

Like all Vermeer's paintings, this one is composed to give a sense of harmony and calm, with strong horizontal, vertical, and diagonal lines.

JEAN-ANTOINE **WATTEAU**   1684–1721 **France**

The Scale of Love 1715–18

Oil on canvas 20 1/2 x 24 in.

Watteau was a French Rococo artist, and the first artist to paint pictures known as "fêtes galantes"—scenes of elegant young people enjoying themselves in the open air. Watteau first made sketches of real men and women, then placed them in fantasy worlds where they wore extravagant costumes and spent their lives having fun.

As the title hints, *The Scale of Love* is a picture about the harmony of music and love. The couple in the foreground is playing a song. Their eyes meet and they lean together so that her music book and his guitar make a bridge between them. As he plays and she sings, we can see that they are a happily matched pair. Behind them, a statue of a philosopher surveys the scene while in the background a group of friends relaxes in the park.

The world-famous Museum of Art was established in 1918 by Mrs. Meg A. Bucks, the millionaire, businessperson, and traveler. An enthusiastic art buyer, Mrs. Bucks spent more than twenty years gathering this wonderful collection of masterpieces from around the world. The Museum of Art prides itself on its reliable staff and friendly atmosphere, so pay us a visit anytime—our doors are open to art lovers everywhere!

PIERO DELLA FRANCESCA

PAOLO **UCCELLO**

HENDRICK **AVERCAMP**

REMBRANDT VAN RIJN

JEAN-BAPTISTE-SIMEON **CHARDIN**

JEAN-BAPTISTE **PERRONNEAU**

THOMAS **GAINSBOROUGH**

PAUL **DELAROCHE**

JEAN-AUGUSTE-DOMINIQUE **INGRES**

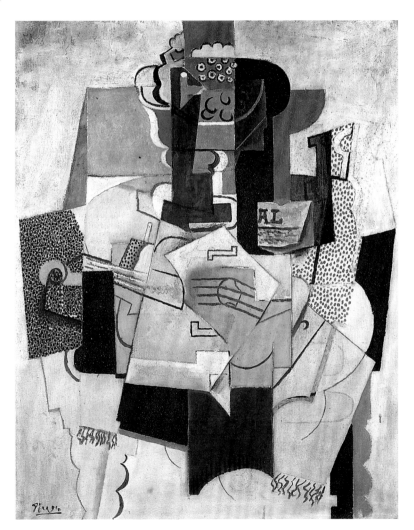

A HELPING HAND

Back in the office, Mr. Bassett has some last minute advice for you....

Have you examined every picture from top to bottom? Do you know which ones are forgeries and which ones are real paintings? Perhaps you want to go back and look at the paintings again? Try finding the symbol first, then look for the changes. Remember that there should be only two artists in each box on your chart—if there are more, you may have missed some changes.

If you are still stuck, don't worry, help is at hand! While you've been busy, I've been doing a bit of detective work myself and have drawn up my own chart. If you need to compare notes, you can use your magnifying glass to check my list.

THE MUSEUM OF ART
CATALOG

GANG SYMBOL / NUMBER OF CHANGES	FISH GANG 🐟	BIRD GANG ✈	STAR GANG ★	TREE GANG ☂
1	RAPHAEL Molly Mullet / CHARDIN Molly Mullet / TURNER Claude Conger	TER BRUGGHEN Gengha Gull / MONET Gengha Gull	VAN OS Portia Pollux / DELAROCHE Portia Pollux	PERRONNEAU Filippi Fig / CONSTABLE Filippi Fig
2	VAN GOGH Claude Conger	PIERO DELLA 3 Lizzie Lapwing / STEENWYCK Lizzie Lapwing	VERMEER Bugsy Betelgeuse / WATTEAU Bugsy Betelgeuse / MASSYS Saffron Sirius	REMBRANDT Annie Apricot / GAINSBOROUGH Annie Apricot / VAN EYCK Josef Juniper
3	BOTTICELLI Bonnie Barracuda / AVERCAMP Bonnie Barracuda	HOLBEIN Hawley Hornbill / DE HOOCH Hawley Hornbill	INGRES Saffron Sirius / GOSSAERT Visèle Vega	SEURAT Josef Juniper / UCCELLO Salome Spruce
4	MARIBUS Attila Archery / ROUSSEAU Attila Archery		DEGAS Visèle Vega	BRUEGHEL Salome Spruce
REAL PAINTINGS (no changes)	1. LEONARDO	2. VAN DE VELDE	3. MORISOT	4. PICASSO

When your chart finally tallies with mine, it's time to call the police. If you have the facts straight, you should be able to prove which fifteen forgers are guilty and identify the mystery caller. I hope you did a good job because the future of the museum is in your hands!

Turn to the next page to see if you have succeeded in bringing the forgers to justice!

THE MOMENT OF TRUTH

VAN EYCK

3 changes 🌴

Josef Juniper

BOTTICELLI

3 changes 🐟

Bonnie Barracuda

MASSYS

3 changes ★

Saffron Sirius

AVERCAMP

3 changes 🐟

Bonnie Barracuda

STEENWYCK

2 changes ✈

Lizzie Lapwing

PIERO

2 changes ✈

Lizzie Lapwing

RAPHAEL

1 change 🐟

Molly Mullet

GOSSAERT

4 changes ★

Vasile Vega

HOLBEIN

3 changes ✈

Hawley Hornbill

TER BRUGGHEN

1 change ✈

Genghis Gull

VAN DE VELDE

No changes

UCCELLO

4 changes 🌴

Salome Spruce

LEONARDO

No changes

MARINUS

4 changes 🐟

Attila Anchovy

BRUEGHEL

4 changes 🌴

Salome Spruce

REMBRANDT

2 changes 🌴

Annie Apricot

Bonnie Barracuda   Molly Mullet   Salome Spruce   Annie Apricot   Portia Pollux   Vasile Vega

Claude Conger   Attila Anchovy   Josef Juniper   Filippi Fig   Saffron Sirius   Bugsy Betelgeuse

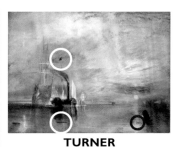

VERMEER

2 changes ★

Bugsy Betelgeuse

PERRONNEAU

1 change ✈

Filippi Fig

VAN OS

1 change ★

Portia Pollux

TURNER

2 changes 🐟

Claude Conger

DEGAS

4 changes ★

Vasile Vega

SEURAT

3 changes ✈

Josef Juniper

DE HOOCH

3 changes ✈

Hawley Hornbill

GAINSBOROUGH

2 changes ✈

Annie Apricot

DELAROCHE

1 change ★

Portia Pollux

INGRES

3 changes ★

Saffron Sirius

MONET

1 change ✈

Genghis Gull

VAN GOGH

2 changes 🐟

Claude Conger

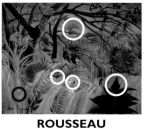

CHARDIN

1 change 🐟

Molly Mullet

WATTEAU

2 changes ★

Bugsy Betelgeuse

CONSTABLE

1 change ✈

Filippi Fig

MORISOT

No changes

ROUSSEAU

4 changes 🐟

Attila Anchovy

PICASSO

No changes

Genghis Gull

Imelda Ibis

Hawley Hornbill

Lizzie Lapwing

Congratulations! You are a top-notch Art Fraud Detective! As you undoubtedly know by now, the paintings by Leonardo, Van de Velde, Morisot, and Picasso are the real masterpieces. Imelda Ibis was the mystery caller—she tipped us off about the other forgers. The police have agreed not to send her to jail, unlike the fifteen guilty forgers. Looks like the pictures will be returned and the museum saved—thanks to you!

GOOD-BYE!

GLOSSARY OF ART TERMS

CANVAS
Until the 1400s, pictures were usually painted on wooden panels. Gradually artists began painting on canvas, a specially prepared cotton fabric. The canvas is stretched on a wooden frame, then painted with a primer to keep the material from absorbing too much paint.

CARTOON
A full-size drawing done in preparation for a painting. The term comes from the Italian word *cartone,* which is used to describe a large sheet of paper.

CLASSICAL
The term used to describe painting or sculpture that is inspired by the pure, simple art of ancient Greece and Rome.

COMPOSITION
The arrangement of objects in a painting or drawing.

CUBISM
A revolutionary art movement started by Picasso and Braque at the beginning of the 1900s. Cubism tried to represent reality in a new way.

FORESHORTENING
In perspective, the technique used to paint an object so that it appears to be three-dimensional.

GOTHIC
A term that describes a style of decorative, courtly painting used in Europe between the late 1300s and the mid-1400s.

IMPRESSIONISM
An art movement of the 1800s. The name comes from Monet's painting, *Impression: Sunrise,* which was exhibited in Paris in 1874 with works by Renoir, Sisley, Cézanne, and Pissarro. These artists wanted to capture the atmosphere and feeling of a scene, rather than just record the accurate, factual details.

LANDSCAPE
A painting of a natural or imaginary outdoor scene.

*The Umbrellas by Renoir
is an Impressionist work.*

OIL PAINT
All paint is made up of powdered pigment (the color), mixed in a liquid called a medium. The medium of oil paint is oil, hence the name. It can be applied with a palette knife or a brush, and first became popular in the 1400s.

PATRON
A person, or a group of people, who buys or commissions art. Some of the most important Renaissance patrons belonged to the wealthy Medici family, a powerful family of bankers who controlled the Italian city of Florence.

PERSPECTIVE
Perspective is a drawing system designed to help a flat, two-dimensional picture look three-dimensional. Faraway objects appear to be smaller than those in the foreground, and all parallel lines traveling away from the viewer seem to meet in the distance at a single "vanishing point." The use of perspective was first seen in the 1400s.

PORTRAIT
A picture of a person, usually drawn from life. A portrait can include just the head

*The Graham Family by Hogarth
is a family portrait.*

and shoulders of one person, or it can show the full figures of a group of people.

RENAISSANCE
The word renaissance means "rebirth." The term is now used to describe an important art movement that took place during the 1400s and 1500s. During this time, artists started to take a great interest in Classical art, and focused on humans as the subject for their paintings and sculptures. Artists such as Raphael, Leonardo da Vinci, and Michelangelo studied anatomy, perspective, and science, all of which gave their art a new, realistic quality. Although the Renaissance started in Italy, it soon spread across Europe.

ROCOCO
A term that describes a style of painting popular in France during the reign of Louis XV (1715–74). These decorative paintings were delicately colored and lighthearted in atmosphere.

STILL LIFE
A painting or drawing of an object or a group of objects, such as pots, utensils, fruit, or flowers.

vanishing point

*This painting of Venice by Canaletto makes
good use of perspective.*

TEMPERA
A type of paint that is made by mixing powdered pigment with a medium of egg. It was the main type of paint used on wooden panels up until the 1400s.

WATERCOLOR
A type of paint that is made by mixing pigment with water.